Curvy (

Awakening My Sexual Desire

Ashley Henry

PUBLISHERS NOTE

First published in the United States of America by

Ashley Henry

Curvy Girls Have Fun Too!

Awakening My Sexual Desire

Ashley Henry

Ashley Henry

SUMMARY

Never Be Afraid To Take a Chance

The protagonist in this story goes through a lot of self discovery. She has had a lot of negativity hurled at her and, in the long run, she is very trusting of men and what they want from her. After she meets a guy through her best friend, she is faced with yet another life changing decision. This time it is different because he has been one of the nicer guys that's he has met. Find out what she decides to do and how things take a positive turn.

ABOUT ASHLEY HENRY

Ashley Henry grew up in a quiet town in Maine with five brothers and sisters. She lived a quiet life until she discovered that her mother was a porn star, well for her father at least. She just happened to see her father watching one of the homemade videos one day. When she asked about it, they were honest and said that they did it because she was proud of her sexuality and it helped her and her husband to keep the spark alive. Ashley was taught to be open to new things.

She carried this with her into adulthood and after completing college she was inspired by her parents to create a story about a girl who was not popular to rise out of that negativity to become more self aware and self confident and to experience love.

Ashley Henry

THE STORY AS IT UNFOLDS...

THE TRUE MEANING OF SEXUAL DISCOVERY

"'Sex' is as important as eating or drinking and we ought to allow the one appetite to be satisfied with as little restraint or false modesty as the other."

Marquis de Sade

DEDICATION

"This is for all the curvy girls who are in a bad place right now. Hold your head up high. People are fickle. Find that confidence to be who you are within yourself. It will make a big difference."

WHO AM I?

I am a twenty-six year old porn star named Joan. I am not the typical star though, not the sexy sirens that you would expect to see on screen. I am a woman that is big and beautiful, a BBW. If that still confuses you, I am fat. There is a market for that kind of porn, just like there is a market for those who like the whips and chains and gay and lesbian sex. I get to have sex with gorgeous guys who would not even look at me twice if they passed me on the street. I just find that extremely interesting and highly ironic. I tend to be repulsive to most yet videos with me and other girls like me in it seem to be getting a big following.

What you may be wondering is how I got into the porn industry? Well let me start from the beginning. I am not that tall, 5' 4" and I am over two hundred pounds. That is quite heavy if you ask me. I have blonde hair and blue eyes. I have huge breasts, 44D. I don't get positive attention when I am out in public; I tend to be the object of ridicule. I learned that early on in life. One guy that I was dating was just doing it to see if I had a pussy that he could find under all the fat.

I was a virgin until I got my shot to be on camera. No guy would touch me like that beforehand. I was used by them to do blowjobs and to jack them off. They had no interest in me being naked or offering them sex as I was just the fat bitch.

As a result of my experiences, I became a bit careful about whom I was with. I never ever got touched, never had a guy eat my pussy or anything like that. I was always the one doing the deed. I was expected to just be happy with the fact that I was allowed to suck their dicks. They had no care or concern for the fact that I was

Ashley Henry

human and that I had feelings. They somehow thought that I was asexual. A lot of people just don't get it that we have feelings.

I really just had to learn how to please myself. I spent most of my time just dealing with my feelings by eating or masturbating. Things started to change in my life however when my friend Phoebe wanted to set me up on a date with a guy she knew named Max. This was about eight months ago.

Now don't get me wrong, porn isn't my major income earner. I do have a regular job. I manage my own bookstore. I pride myself in sourcing hard to find books for my customers. Max was a friend that Phoebe had met in college. He had introduced her to the boyfriend she had had in college. She was visiting me at the bookstore one day when he happened to walk in and saw us talking. He had not seen her for a while and when he had a chance, he grabbed her to find out who I was and how he could meet me. I found that a bit odd as I remember everyone that comes in the store. It is not that big and I did not remember him at all. Curiosity got the better of me however and I decided to meet him and see what exactly he wanted.

I would be extremely cautious as I knew men did not find me that sexy. If it worked out, it worked out. I don't think Phoebe would put me in any situation where I would get hurt as she was always looking out for me. If he did not like me, I would be okay. I had no grand expectations. I expected nothing from it. I was used to going home and masturbating with my favorite vibrator. That was always there for me.

MEETING HIM

I got a call that same evening from Max. I wish I had done some research on him or I would have made different choices. I spoke to him, he was pleasant enough and then we agreed to meet after work on Friday. I was aware that he already knew what I looked like. I just could not figure out why he wanted to go out with me, I was one hundred plus pounds overweight. He must be a brave one to want to be seen out with me.

So he came to the bookstore after work and after I locked up, we headed to a cafe nearby. We had something to eat and then we headed to the movies. I was given the option to choose what I wanted to see. We could not talk much during the movie but that went okay.

I expected that would be it but he asked me if I wanted to have a few drinks and chat some more. I found that strange but I agreed and he took me to a bar. We got to know each other. I was not really sharing a lot of info. He told me owned a small company that filmed documentaries. His major in college had been film. That was okay, I thought to myself.

It was a field that I had always been interested in. I just sat and listened to him gush about what he did and how things really worked in that industry. He was probably being modest by saying that he was not really earning a lot. He said he had to do other projects to earn enough to pay his bills.

He then turned his attention toward me, wanting to know how I came to own the bookstore and what else I did. My life really was not that interesting but he seemed captivated when I was talking about it. I was really a boring person. The only fun times I had were

Ashley Henry

with Phoebe when we went out. He was curious about why I had never considered being in film myself as I was a pretty girl and I had a bubbly personality. I wondered why he would ask as I did not have much experience in the field. I had no links in the industry so who the heck would want a fat person on their team. It was as if I had thrown him a hook with bait on it. All of a sudden he was interested in helping me get into the industry. He knew lots of people who were okay with people my size. They did not discriminate.

I was of course interested as he was not very specific about what type of role I would play or what I would be acting in. I was not thinking it was anything beyond the norm. After leaving the bar he dropped me home and escorted me to the door. I was still wary about why he was not running for the hills yet but the date had gone very well.

He was very nice. We got to my door and he did something I did not expect. He actually kissed me. It was a real kiss with tongue action. He caught me off guard. He was gently caressing me as he kissed me. I could not breathe, was he serious or just warming me up to suck his dick before he kicked me to the curb. I would enjoy whatever this was while it lasted. He was handsome and he was kissing me. I decided to test him so I asked him if he would like to come in for a bit, have some coffee or tea. He was okay with that.

LOSING MY VIRGINITY

We went in and he started to kiss me again as soon as I closed the door. He was very gentle and was not forcing himself on me at all. I actually could feel his dick and it was hard. This was real; he really did feel something for me. I was getting all excited. My pussy muscles were contracting and releasing and I was getting wet. If this did not go any further, I would live. I could give him a hand job or blowjob as he had been nice all evening.

So we never had any coffee or tea. He asked me to carry him to my bedroom. I was game so I did. He started to caress me all over. He had his hands on my boobs. He also put his hand up my skirt and was squeezing my ass. This was the most I had ever gotten from a guy. I unbuckled his belt and zipped his pants down, taking his semi hard dick out. I would thank him for the evening all right. I went down on my knees and started to suck his dick. I was pretty good at it with all my prior experience.

This one I would not regret. He stopped me though just when I expected him to deposit his seed in my mouth. He helped me up and helped me take off my dress and then he put me to sit on the bed; another first for me; a man wanting to see me out of clothing. He pulled my bra and pulled my panties down. I was now totally naked. I was suddenly shy.

He did not seem to be disgusted. Instead he had me sit on the bed. He started to kiss me all over. He sucked on my breasts and went all the way down to my pussy. I was losing my mind. Was this just a big joke? He seemed serious enough and judging by his erect dick, I assumed he was interested.

"Ah, Max, I have never had sex before. I... I..."

"That's okay. Do you want me to just eat your pussy then so you can maintain that?"

"I know we just met but heck no. I want you to fuck me."

"Only if you are sure Joan; don't make a hasty decision because you are all heated."

"I am sure Max. This is the last night of being a virgin for me."

He took that answer. He undressed quickly and then he reached into his pants pocket and got out a condom. Nice he came prepared.

He gently pushed me so I would lie down on the bed. He sucked on my breasts again sending shivers through my body. He moved down until he got to my pussy again. He spread my legs apart and he started to eat me. I was feeling so many different sensations; I did not know what to do with myself. I was enjoying this. It was much better when someone else did it. I hoped I was not too sweaty. He was not stopping. He kept on eating me. I was shaking as he sucked on my clit. I was nervous and excited all at the same time.

I was moaning getting louder as his sucking intensified. I was shaking so bad. So this is what it feels like to have someone give you pleasure. I lost all sense of self when I hit that crescendo. I came hard. That was my first courtesy of a man. He looked up smiling.

"I think you are ready to be deflowered now."

He slipped on the condom and came over me. He entered me slowly, taking his time as I was a newbie. I was not in pain but the pressure was crazy. He stopped to let my pussy adjust to the size of his dick. He kept doing that, getting further in each time. Soon he was pushing against my hymen. He was being so gentle. He was clearly a pro at this. He kissed me and said,

"I am going to push a bit harder now so brace yourself, this will hurt a bit."

"I don't care! I want you to fuck me."

He started to push hard. He kept pushing until my hymen popped. I strangely did not feel much pain. That was it, virgin no more. He started to fuck me now. He kept on fucking me until I came again and then he came shortly after. I was now a woman as they say. Losing my virginity to him was a very enjoyable and thrilling experience.

I expected him to find some excuse to leave but he stayed put. He was curious about how I felt now that I was no longer a virgin. I was okay with it. I was old enough and I wanted to be deflowered a long time ago. I just could not any interested party to help me. He kissed me and started to tell me how sexy I was and that he really loved my body. He was not for real. Maybe all of this was a dream. I had fallen and hit my head and was in a coma having this experience. I would wake up in hospital and realize it soon enough.

"Max, I have to ask you something. You have been complementing me ever since we met. Is it that you like fat girls like me or something? Is that your fetish?"

"I like girls of all sizes but the bigger ones really turn me on."

"Okay, I appreciate that. I am happy I went out with you tonight and I do not regret losing my virginity to you."

Ashley Henry
"How did you remain a virgin for so long Joan? You are gorgeous?"

Wow, he sure could drop those compliments. What did he really want from me? I would just have to be bold and find out. I was a really big girl. He was up to something.

Curvy Girls Have Fun Too!

MAKING THE OFFER

"Okay Max, you have been extremely nice to me. That I find weird. Can you tell me what you really want from me other than the sex you just got? I am a big girl, I can take it.

He sighed and said, "Well, I had told you that I was doing other jobs to get by. One of them is filming for the adult industry, you know porn films. I am working on a project now which is exclusive for me who love big girls like you, you know the BBW (big beautiful woman). We post everything online and customers pay to view out videos. We find women and interview then to see if they are suitable and then if they are we get things rolling."

And there it was. He had basically just checked me out to see if I would be suitable to be in one or more of these porn flicks.

"Okay so that is it. So why didn't you just ask me upfront to be a slut for your personal gain?" After such a nice evening, I was more than a bit upset.

He could tell that I was pissed.

"I am sorry Joan. I really enjoyed being out with you tonight. I really think you are gorgeous. I just see how you would sizzle in front of those cameras."

I was pissed but receptive. I sat there in silence, thinking. He realized that I was not running him out of my home just yet so he decided to try something else.

"Alright, how about I show you what we post online and you can decide what you what to do. Even if you don't want to, I would still be interested in seeing you. I really like you."

16

Ashley Henry

That was a really weird way to give out a compliment. He went for my laptop and got back in bed with me. He went to the website and I had a look at it. You could view various profiles of these BBWs and select who you wanted to watch, the pictures had them in various poses. Some were being fucked, some were sucking dick and some were being eaten. I found it all to be extremely exciting. I never knew that websites like this existed anywhere at all. He let me go through the tour so I could see everything that they had to offer.

"So all these women are not professional porn stars?"

"No, we are always seeking new talent. Some stay on and take it on as a profession. Others do it for a short time for the thrill or just o make some extra cash for something specific."

The aim is to have women on that did not seem too aloof that they would never be Available to some men.

"So who are the men? Where do you find them?"

"Oh, that is easy. I am one and the other men are my colleagues. If you are interested you are paid per session so even if you try it and hate it, you can always get out. I honestly think that you could be a big star like Jenna Jameson."

"Honestly Max, do people really pay for this kind of pornography?"

"Yes, they do and the demand is increasing. We have been putting out good stuff and people are beginning to notice. If you are worried that you won't be treated well, don't. We are all extremely nice and we like what we do. If you don't want to be recognized, we can do a wig and makeup to alter your appearance."

I sighed. He was done talking. He took the laptop and put it on the floor beside the bed. He started to kiss me again, teasing my nipples with his fingers. I gasped. It was kind of hard to think while he did that. He was getting hard again. He jumped out of the bed and grabbed another condom. I was sore but would not mind him fucking me again. He slipped the condom on and he pushed his dick into my pussy. He fucked me a bit harder than the first time. I was still super tight and the tenderness made me feel a new sensation. I was panting loudly pretty quickly. I came pretty quickly. He kept on thrusting in me until he came. He was sweaty and exhausted.

After asking me to think about it, he got dressed and he left saying he would contact me to find out what my decision was.

I had time to bask in the fact that I was sexually liberated. I also had time to think about the proposal that he had made. I was still thinking that it was all so surreal. He's as a very nice looking man and he had picked me out and fucked me in the hopes of getting me to do porn for him. I enjoyed the fucking and I stood to gain from it. I had also learned that there was a market out there for fat women who were willing to have sex on camera, women who had no problem with their size.

I lay in the bed, thinking about the prospect of having men who looked as nice as him or even nicer having sex with me. I could see myself on set, under all those lights as the star of the show. It was a sexually stimulating thought.

I would seriously be thinking about doing this. The extra money would not hurt and I was going to get to have lots of great sex. I would fuck Max again. I really liked how gentle he was with me initially. He understood me and somehow knew how to fulfill my needs. There must be something he hadn't mentioned but I just could not figure it out. All I really knew is that a handsome man saw me naked and got a hard on twice in one night and fucked me twice in one night.

Of course there were negatives to all of this. I would be naked in front of God knows how many people. I don't know if I would be able to deal with that and as thrilling as the thought was, would I really be able to have sex in that situation. I was new to sex, would I do okay. Despite the wig and makeup, someone might just figure out that it was me on the website and I would be ruined. I would not be able to conduct any business without being the object of speculation. It could all end up turning out really badly for me.

I would look at the website again. I still had access to it so I could browse. It was all a part of his plan I suppose to get me to take the bait. The women were ordinary enough. I wondered why they did it, other than for money. It could be the thrill that someone would watch them. I could have even passed some of these women on the street and not know what they really did.

I was still battling with the thought that fat women were a commodity. From what was on the website, it was apparently true. One thing that I saw ring true was that it was the same set of men all the time. They must be stallions to be having so much sex. The women were treated extremely well. It was not about mocking them or humiliating them. Everyone seemed to be enjoying what was going on. What would I really do? For now I would sleep. I got out of the bed, changed the sheets, had a quick shower and went back to bed. I was asleep in no time. I was sexually exhausted.

Taking Things Into Consideration

I avoided Max's calls and he was respectful enough to not come stalk me at the bookstore. He gave me the time to think about whether or not I wanted to be in these films. I let the thought simmer. I did not call him until about two weeks after.

"Hello Joan, I was really hoping that you would call."

"I am not saying yes yet. I want to know if I can get a tour of your facility so I can get a true feel for what you really do."

"I would be happy to do that."

He gave me the address on the building that they filmed in and told me that I would be able to come there on Saturday. I told him thanks and that I would see him then. They start filming really early in the morning so I was up and out do the house before 7 am. I got there on time and rang the bell. A guy answered. I hesitated and asked if this is where Max worked. He smiled and stepped aside to let me in.

"Come on, you are in the right place. Max told me to expect you. I hope you take up the offer."

"We will see." I said.

"Great, come on, you can meet everybody before we start. I am Richard by the way."

He was one of the guys that I had seen on the website. We went in and I met the other men Chad, Jeffrey and Dylan. They did everything it seems as they worked the lights cameras plus acted on screen except for Dylan. He was the technological guru. He was the webmaster and he made sure all the equipment was in good working order. He was not much of a talker it seemed as after meeting me he rushed off to keep on checking the equipment. They would be starting in ten minutes so everybody was busy. I squeezed myself into a corner, to keep out of everyone's way. I looked at the set. It was nice, just like a modern home with living room, kitchen and bedroom.

I saw Max come in. he smiled when he saw me and he came over to say hello. He gave me a kiss and took my hand.

"I am in charge of filming today so you can stick with me and get a firsthand look at how we do things here ok."

"So where is the girl that will be filmed today?"

"Oh, she is still getting ready. She is in another room, having her makeup done."

I kept on looking around. I took a seat and waited. Soon enough I saw two BBWs approaching. One was Felecia, she was being filmed today. She was actually fatter than I with humungous boobs that she has squeezed into a bustier of sorts. She was dressed in sexy lingerie and ready to go. The other woman was Amanda. She was the makeup artist.

They were ready. Max was talking.

"Okay everyone; we are ready, places please. Felecia, I have never seen you look so beautiful."

The lights were set, boom ready, actors in place. They just needed Max to give them the go ahead. Felecia seemed to be a bit nervous.

Curvy Girls Have Fun Too!

"Okay, let's do the interview. Remember to follow the prompter Felecia. Just keep going no matter what. We need it to look natural."

"Alright," Felecia said.

"Quiet on the set," Max bellowed. "Three, two, one... ACTION!"

It started off with Felecia alone on camera. Richard was asking her questions. He asked her what her name was, how tall she was, how much she weighed, pretty standard questions. She gave her stage name as "Xena". She was two hundred and thirty pounds. You could see that she was a novice but that made everything more believable.

Richard then got to the meat of the matter. He wanted to know about her sex life, what she liked to do in bed. She answered and suddenly she started to feel herself. She was pinching her nipples. Richard offered to assist her and after she said yes, he was beside her, helping her. He was squeezing her breasts. Soon he started to kiss her and he was caressing her all over. The scene just progressed like that.

She was moaning and responding to his touch.

"Hmmm "Xena", I love these big boobs." Richard said.

She moaned in response. She was a lot less nervous now as she let him turn her on. He took of some of what she had on leaving her in a sexy lace panty. She was a real fat girl like me indeed, with folds of skin and stretch marks to boot.

Richard's hands were all over her. She turned and bent over so her butt was in the frame. Richard was looking at it and licking his lips. He slapped her a few times on the ass lightly, making the fat jiggle.

"I want to see more "Xena"."

With that said, he pulled her panties to one side, revealing her ass and her pussy. I could see that the camera man for today Jeffrey was shooting from specific angle so "Xena" was looking great when you looked on the monitor.

Richard kept rubbing her ass and then he slowly slid one finger into her pussy and played with her a bit. She was wet already. He removed his finger and started to get undressed. She started to turn slowly.

"CUT." Max said.

I wondered why he said this as things were just starting to get interesting. I soon found out why. Richard taking off clothes was not what the viewer wanted to see plus it would cut back on cost and time spent editing. Richard was undressed quickly enough and I also saw that he was aroused. Felecia was now totally naked as well. I also saw that the woman who had been introduced as the makeup person Amanda was also taking off her clothes. What role would she play?

"Felecia, you can start the blowjob on Richard now, we will just start filming again and I will stop you when we have enough."

She sat down and started to suck Richard's dick.

He held his hand up and everyone was quiet again. "ACTION!"

23

Curvy Girls Have Fun Too!

I noticed that Max kept a keen eye on the monitor. Jeffrey was doing close ups of this scene. She was pretty good. She was working the head of his dick in her mouth while working the shaft with her hand. She was working hard, making noise as she sucked him. Soon she was told to stop and change position. She was now on her knees.

We could see her face now. Richard slipped on a condom and was ready to enter her from behind.

They started filming again and Richard pushed his dick slowly into "Xena" and then he started to fuck her. He kept the hand closest to the camera back so he would not be blocking anything. Jeffrey zoomed as the fucking intensified. It was a good thing the focus was on Felicia's rear end as she had a quizzical expression on her face. Jeffrey was really zooming in, giving the soon to be viewers their money's worth.

Soon he was instructed to pan to her face and then to focus on her big tits that were jumping. The sound was turned off and he instructed Felecia to look like she was getting the best fuck that she had ever had. She was also to moan and make it sound really good.

The sound was back on and they shot that scene. She got into it. She was moaning and looking as if she was totally in ecstasy. The focus was on the tits and the face. I also realized what Amanda was doing. She was sitting on a chair so Richard could see her. She had her legs wide open and she was masturbating for him. That was a bit puzzling to me. I learned later on that she was the "fluffer" and she was to do that to help Richard or any male actor that was being filmed to remain aroused. I guess it was hard to focus on the act of sex itself with all the directions being given.

Ashley Henry

Amanda also went on set when the filming was stopped to help keep him erect as well. She would massage him and suck his dick until he was fully erect again. As soon as she was done, the filming resumed. "Xena" was just there to be fucked and to look as if she loved it. Even at the end of it all, Amanda would perform fellatio until he was about to cum and then she would stop and he would pull the condom off and jack off, spraying his cum onto "Xena's" ass. She then reached back and rubbed it in.

They then went back into some interview process where Richard complemented her on her performance, asked what she thought of the experience and if she would be willing to return. After that they were done.

Amanda was fully dressed again and she gave the actor towels. Max was telling everyone they did a great job, especially Felecia who he gave a big hug and a kiss. She and Richard then went off to shower.

I mean, it was okay for what it was but because of all the stops and directions being given, I found it less than stimulating.

"You would never think that all of that had to happen to make the perfect porn flick did you?" Max said. "We create a masterpiece from all of this, something that looks flawless and not tampered with."

He was right. The viewers had no idea that this is what went on behind the scenes. I mean Felecia did not even have an orgasm. How do you really deal with that? I had to give the actors kudos for that, to remain focused in such a situation. The men had to really focus to pull it off. They could fuck a rubber pussy for all we knew. It just had to be properly lubricated. In all honesty, it was something I could do. I just had to decide if I was up to it or not.

25

Curvy Girls Have Fun Too!

I spoke to everyone to get an even better understanding of what was happening. I was soon ready to leave. I was shocked that Dylan actually came over to tell me goodbye. He was really nice.

Ashley Henry

MAKING MY DECISION

I went back home and after grabbing some lunch, I sat and thought about it. I was just coming to the realization that I had just had access to the set of a pornographic shoot. They were not the big business porn company but they were doing all right. The filming was great as they highlighted all of Felecia best qualities on film. They made use of the various angles so she was always looking spectacular.

I would love to see what the finished product would look like. That would really give me better insight; I probably would have made my decision by then anyway. I was a bit more comfortable with the prospect of doing something like this. I liked that only the essential people were there when shooting was taking place and I liked it that everyone was respectful. There was no mocking of fat girls or anyone else on this set. By the time the sun set I knew what I would do. I would do it.

I did not call Max right away. I called him mid week, in the afternoon to let him know that I would not have a problem being filmed like that.

"Oh. Joan, dear Joan, I am really happy that you are saying yes to this. Hmmm I would love to film you next Saturday morning. Let me know if that will be okay for you. You can have someone else open the bookstore like you did when you came to see what we did."

"Yes, I can ask Phoebe. I can't tell her why though. I will just say I have an appointment or something."

Curvy Girls Have Fun Too!

I marked the day on my calendar. I would not see my period until the next week so I was good.

"So what do I need to do beforehand to prepare?"

"Let's see, you should come in comfortable dressed so wear like a pair of sweats and a big shirt or something. Just make sure it is not tight."

I did not have to do much else as Amanda would do the makeup, help me with my wig and also trim or wax my pubic hair. Okay this was easy so far, I would let Amanda wax me clean or maybe leave a pattern in the middle. I had always wanted to do that but really had no reason to, until now.

I had really matured. I was talking about having sex on camera with someone who I had just had sex once with. Wow! I just hoped that no one I knew was into this sort of porn.

"Oh there is one more thing that you can do beforehand. Do take a nice relaxing bath. Use some scented oils or something so you smell great all over. Remember that one of us will be all over you. It is much better if you smell nice all over. Some women don't get that at all."

He also gave me a synopsis of where I would be filmed. I would get to go in the bedroom first. I would go through the same interview process at the start then I would be fucked all over the place and then after I would go through the exit interview which would let the viewers know if they would see me again. I was also asked to come up with a name for the character I would play. I thought for a bit and decided on Dayna. It would do. Max was okay with that. He took my email address and said he would send me some additional info. We rang off.

Ashley Henry

I got through the rest of the work day and as soon as I got home, I made a cup of tea and checked my email. It outlined what the basic script was and it also explained how the camera shots were done and when exactly they would zoom in and zoom out and so on the emphasis was placed on why the "money shots" were important. Those included me with a fully erect dick in my mouth or an erect dick being pushed into my pussy. I also only did the interview only once. After that it was just a scenario that I would act out that would lead to sex. It was all pretty easy to understand. I just hoped that I did not botch it by being too nervous.

I could barely get through the rest of the week as I was starting to get butterflies in my stomach. Even Phoebe could tell that something was giving me the jitters.

"Hey Joan, what's up with you? You have been on pins and needles all week."

"Oh, I am fine."

"But you look so flushed. Are you getting sick or something?"

"No I am peachy." I could not tell her that I was going to be sucking dick and taking cock this weekend.

I excused myself and went off to do sort out some shelves on the other side of the store.

I was having the jitters really bad and needless to say that I had changed my mind a hundred times since I had the conversation with Max. It is just that he took my virginity and opened up the sexy side of me. I wanted to really explore that side of my persona. I was not yet at the stage where sex was just plain old sex. I was still excited by the thought of it. After all I was fresh into the

Curvy Girls Have Fun Too!
experience. Of course the filming process would be different but I would find a way to have my moment. I convinced myself that I had made the right decision.

Ashley Henry

THE DAY OF THE SHOOT

It was Saturday and I was up really early. I took my time with my bath, getting into every nook and cranny. I then reviewed the information that Max had emailed to me. After having something to eat, I brushed and flossed like my life depended on it. I got dressed putting on a pair of sweats and the accompanying hoodie. I remembered that I was not to wear any underwear. In fact I did not sleep in any the night before, just to ensure that I would have those telltale panty lines on my skin.

I had already gotten waxed as I was so excited about that. I had a lightning bolt going down the middle. I thought that it was extremely sexy. I was going to make sure that I rushed into the building that they filmed in and that no one saw me coming out. I was not even going to drive just in case someone passing by recognized the car.

I was ready. I left the house and headed toward my first day on the job as a porn star. I got there in record time and knocked on the door. Richard greeted me again. He was all smiles.

"You have a big day ahead of you, don't you? How are you feeling about it?"

"I am okay for now I guess," I answered nervously.

He rubbed my shoulder. "Don't worry, you will be fine. Just go down the hall and go into the second room. Amanda is already there waiting on you. She has your outfit and will help with your makeup."

I found the room and with her expert help I was dressed and ready pretty quickly. I went to the set and everyone was busy don't the
31

final checks. I felt like there was a rock in the pit of my stomach. I had to do what I was supposed to or all of their efforts would be in vain.

I knew how important I was in the whole deal. I was grateful that Max was confident in me to allow me to do that. I was not doing a major blockbuster film or anything like that but I had a major part to play and I would give it my best shot. My body would be the main focus and it would be displayed well, thanks to the camera man. I was appreciated because of the size I was and not the opposite of that which I had gotten used to. Amanda was coming back to me.

"Hey Joan you will be fine, don't look so worried. Come sit here and relax. The guys are really professional. I am sure you saw that when you came here. Do you have your own lube or do you need me to bring some for you?"

I indicated that I had some.

"Okay when we are ready to go, I will help you to lube up as I don't want you to use too much."

She was very nice and made sure that I was okay and that everything was in place for me. I couldn't have asked for better help.

"Okay girl, it's almost show time. It is time to take your clothes off."

I got undressed. She looked me over and smiled and started to apply my makeup.

"So you look pretty neat. Do you always do this?"

"No, I choose to wax a few days ago before the shoot."

"That was a great choice. It works out better in the long run."

She was really good at makeup application. I almost did not recognize myself. She made me look like a sex goddess and it was not too gaudy. She tucked my real hair into a wig cap and then put me in a red wig. I was a siren. I really looked different.

"Yup, you are more than ready; you will be with Chad today. We will start shooting in the next few minutes."

She then helped me lube out and handed me a sexy red thong. I strangely did not feel awkward with her lubing me up. I slipped the thong on. Next she went and got a gorgeous silver gown to put on. It fit perfectly. I slipped on a pair of matching silver slippers and I was ready.

Sex On Camera

I took a deep breath. I was about to start filming my first porn movie. This would be the second time, well third as he had fucked me two times on the first night that I would have a man's dick in my pussy. I could hardly believe it.

I was in place now, ready to be interviewed and Max and crew were all ready.

"Okay people, three, two, one...Action!" Max said.

The cameras were rolling and all eyes were on me. Chad was in his spot off camera and he was going through the routine questions.

"Hello gorgeous, what is your name?"

"I'm Dayna," I said.

"So why are you here today?"

"I am here to audition for BBWs on Fire," I responded.

"Fantastic, you are really beautiful."

"Thanks," I said giving what I thought was my most seductive smile.

They had put me to sit on the edge of the bed and I had my legs crossed with my hands on my lap. I could barely see anyone behind the bright lights but they were all busy. Chad went on asking questions.

"So, Dayna, how old are you?"

Ashley Henry
"I am twenty-six years old.

"Nice, how much do you weigh and how tall are you?

"Well I am 5' 4" and I weigh two hundred and fifteen pounds."

"I love it and I think that you are extremely sexy."

"So are you a sexual woman?"

"I would like to think so."

The questions went on. I had to say what positions I liked best and what I liked to do. On cue, I started to undress for him, just a teaser of course. I shifted the straps and let the dress drop so that my breasts were visible. He of course asked to help and after I agreed he was right there with me. He started to kiss me while caressing my breasts.

I smiled at him, "I like that."

He kept on kissing me moving down until a nipple was in his mouth. I started to caress him as well playing with his nipples and going down until I my hand my hand on his dick. I was actually enjoying his lips on my breasts. He shifted so I could get in his pants. Soon I had his dick in hand.

"Ooohhh," I said seductively, "I am going to enjoy this."

I started to suck his dick. It was larger than Max's own and I was thrilled. He was actually hard. I gave him my best blowjob ever.

"He was enjoying it as he could not help moaning. I knew it was real. Soon I heard Max say cut. At that point Chad and I got out of our clothes.
35

Filming started back with me continuing to suck his dick. He held my hair back so it would not obscure the view. I could taste the pre-cum coming out of his dick. Soon we changed positions. He went back to kissing me all over. I was enjoying it and so I gave it my all. Soon he had my ass facing the camera. He pulled the thong down to reveal my well lubed pussy. He had his finger in.

I was really getting into it. Next I was having my breast sucked again while he played with my clit, spreading the lips of my pussy so that what he was doing could clearly be seen. That required a close up.

I was following the script to a T, not missing a beat. I was not even nervous. I was moaning appropriately, just loud enough for the noise to be picked up but not too loud. After the cameraman got all the shots it was time to get to the meat of the matter. I was on my knees with my big ass sticking up. I was set at the right angle so that everything would be seen. I was actually wet; I probably would not have to use lube next time.

Following the script, I put a hand through my legs to rub my own clit while Chad got his condom on. He then entered me from behind, slowly for effect. I gasped as he was really big and I was still extremely tight. I knew he felt it too. He started to fuck me now while I moaned and groaned for the camera. I must be captivating as Amanda did not have to do her off screen masturbation at all. Chad had remained hard just from what I was doing. He was one who just loved sex with all types of women, like Max.

I kept to my lines, what I could remember of them as he was having an effect on me. Chad was really into it now. He was going full throttle. This must look good on camera. I would have to watch it and see how I did and how I looked being fucked from behind. It was a first for me. That turned me on even more.

36

Ashley Henry

He pulled out. He was sweaty. I was now to be on top. I marveled at his bravery. He hopped on the bed and I straddled him. I lowered myself onto his dick. He had me lean forward so that the camera could pick up his dick going in and out of my pussy. He was nibbling on my nipples.

"Oh yeah," I said, "fuck me hard."

"Oh you hot bitch, I love being in your tight pussy."

We shifted again with him on top, thrusting into me. After a few minutes I heard cut again. I was now to get in position for the cum shot. He would cum in my face. I was kneeling on the bed and he was over me. He pulled off the condom. After rubbing some lube on he was ready. After getting the go ahead he started stroking his cock. It did not take long for him to cum, shooting his think cum all over my face. I had my mouth open to catch what I could. When he was done he let me suck the rest off.

He then thanked me and told me that I was perfect for the job. I responded with a grateful smile while I caressed my breasts and that was a wrap.

Max was ecstatic. Everyone was clapping. It had been a great shoot.

"I told you that you had a knack for it." He gave me a kiss on the cheek.

I was happy but still felt as if I was missing something as I had not cum. I was still heated. I had to masturbate in the shower before I left. I was proud of myself though. I had something in public that I thought that I would never do in a million years. I felt empowered.

AFTER

I handed Amanda the wig and headed to the shower. Chad was through pretty quickly and gave me a quick kiss before grabbing his towel and leaving. I was alone in the bathroom. I could finish the job now. I let the warm water run over me while I started to rub my clit. I was so focused on what I was doing that I did not realize that someone had come into the bathroom and was standing behind me.

I felt a gentle touch on my shoulder and I turned around. It was Max and he was naked, dick saluting me. He already had on a condom. He kissed me deeply.

"I knew you would be great. I was so turned on."

With that he started to caress me all over. I leaned forward and placed my hands on the wall to support myself. My legs were open and he came up behind me and entered me. He was fucking me hard in no time. I could not hold in the moans. I was off camera and we were alone. I pushed back against him as he fucked me. It did not take long for me to cum. My body shook all over. He came pretty quickly too as he had been really turned on by what I did on screen.

"Wow Joan, It is not good to mix business with pleasure but I will have to make an exception for you."

We washed off together and he left me to dry off and get dressed.

I must say that the video I did got a lot of hits. I was a popular girl and had a loyal following pretty quickly. In the eight months that I have been filming porn I have done over twelve shoots. The great thing is that I get to have fun on screen with whoever I am acting with and I get to have more fun off screen with Max. I loved my part time job. It was extremely rewarding in more ways than one. I have had a serious boost in self esteem since I started. I can proudly say that curvy girls have fun too!

Curvy Girls Have Fun Too!

CPSIA information can be obtained
at www.ICGtesting.com
Printed in the USA
LVHW040821181222
735461LV00008B/878

CPSIA information can be obtained
at www.ICGtesting.com
Printed in the USA
LVHW040821181222
735461LV00008B/878

9 781681 276649